Hood

Hunting falcon

Hunting falcon

Falcon-hunting

Arrows

knightly protect ak against ce!

Hunting bow

Quiver

Keys

Armor gauntlets

Chest for valuables

Dagger with sheath

n of e this

Salve for wounds

Bandage

Pine torch

Healing herbs

Knife

Eating utensil

Learned book

Pine torch holder

My knight Frank is the bravest knight in all the West

Many thanks to my co-workers Vinzenz, Veronika, Joseph, and Reinhard

Ali Mitgutsch
A Knight's Book

The adventures of Squire Wolflieb and his knight, Sir Frank von Fidelstein

Translated from the German by Elizabeth D. Crawford

Clarion Books

New York

Clarion Books
a Houghton Mifflin Company imprint
215 Park Avenue South, New York, NY 10003
Copyright © 1990 by Ravensburger Buchverlag Otto Maier GmbH
Original German title: RITTERBUCH
English translation copyright © 1991 by Elizabeth D. Crawford

Library of Congress Cataloging-in-Publication Data
Mitgutsch, Ali.
[Ritterbuch. English]
A knight's book / Ali Mitgutsch ; translated by Elizabeth D. Crawford.
p.   cm.
Translation of: Ritterbuch.
Summary: Young Wolflieb relates the medieval adventures of his
poor but brave master, Sir Frank von Fidelstein, such as participating
in a tournament and fighting a duel.
ISBN 0-395-58103-6
[1. Knights and knighthood—Fiction.   2. Civilization, Medieval—
Fiction.]   I. Title.
PZ7.M6995Kn 1991
[Fic]—dc20   90-20858
CIP
AC

10 9 8 7 6 5 4 3 2 1

Begin at the beginning, you say, but that would take a very long time, and you'd be tired before I got to the interesting part. I'll tell you about the time I went on my first journey away from home, with my knight, Sir Frank von Fidelstein. It was many years ago, but I remember it all as clearly as if it were happening now.

We'd been traveling for three days of rain through desolate country. No friendly castle, no inn where a person could get warm and dry. I was used to it, for we were poor. My knight, Sir Frank, was poor, and I was poor too. I didn't even have any shoes. I swore that one day I'd be a great knight, and a rich one, and then I would never, ever leave my castle when it was raining. I'd sit by the fire in my castle and toast my toes.

The knights of Fidelstein were always the bravest in battle. But when it came to dividing the spoils of war, others were always quicker than they. And so my knight's castle was high in the mountains, where the land is poor and not much will grow. The farmers who tilled his fields in return for his protection had almost nothing to give him. They were poor and thin. Everyone was thin—the farmers, their wives, the children, the men at arms, the squires, our horse, and the knight of Fidelstein himself.

Sir Frank didn't look very impressive in his mended clothes and his comical helm that our village smith welded together from old bits and pieces. But in spite of all that, and even when he was wandering around in the rain, my Sir Frank was still the bravest knight in the whole Western world.

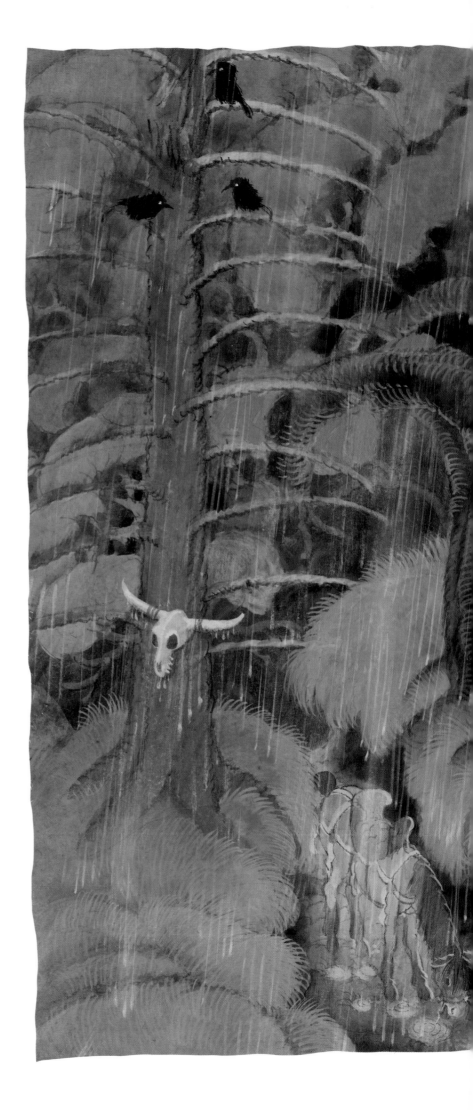

We were on the way to the mighty fortress of Stolzenfels. There was going to be a tremendous tournament there the next week. Sir Frank wanted to try his skill in battle against the other knights. The victors would win fame and glory and perhaps even a prize.

By rights we should have reached our destination much earlier, but we got lost and were wandering around this gigantic forest, when we could have been in out of the rain long before. The roads were bad, and there weren't any signposts, either.

My Sir Frank was far from being afraid, and I admired his courage. Courage was the best thing about us—courage and my name, Wolflieb, which means "dear to the wolf." Wolflieb was a name invented just for me. My father wanted to call me Wolfgang after his father, but my mother wanted to call me Gottlieb after her brother. They couldn't agree, so they combined both names, and the result was the wonderful name of Wolflieb. Wolflieb von Wolfenstein! Now that's a real name! I dreamed of the day when I would have a castle and be a great, powerful knight.

Finally things began to get better. The rain stopped, we happened onto a proper road, and suddenly we were among people. They were knights with their squires and men at arms, all on the way to Stolzenfels Castle! We already knew some of them, and loud greetings were exchanged. We scarcely noticed that the forest was growing lighter and the heavens brighter. When we passed beneath a large oak and out of the woods, the valley and the castle of Stolzenfels lay before us.

Many colored tents had already been put up around the tournament grounds. There were pennons and banners flying, a busy to-ing and fro-ing everywhere, and the sounds of calls and laughter, the hammering of smiths, and the music of bagpipes, cornet, and fiddle.

Famous—and very wealthy—knights were arriving with crowds of attendants, men at arms, cooks, personal weapon-smiths, and scribes. Other knights had bonesetters and healers with them.

And there were many vagrant people! These are people outside the law, who have no one to protect them. They must either protect themselves or ask for the protection of someone more powerful than they.

The bear trainers made their bears dance. The acrobats walked along a high rope without falling. Jugglers whirled two, three, even five balls through the air at the same time. There were the little old women who will read the future for a coin. Their kettles bubbled with secret herbal brews that have the power to heal.

Since we didn't have our own tent, we arranged straw mattresses in a side building of the castle, where we'd be sheltered from the rain and wind.

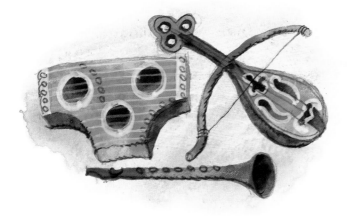

After I'd taken care of our faithful horse Tristrud, I went to collect brushwood for the communal campfire. Suddenly I heard the angry barking of dogs in the thicket and an anxious voice calling for help. Armed with a cudgel, I beat my way through the bushes. The racket got louder and louder. In a clearing I saw a girl. She was trying to fend off a gang of dogs, but the branch she'd armed herself with was rotten. With each blow the branch got a little bit shorter. I made my voice very deep and, bellowing fiercely, rushed at the dogs. I laid about with my cudgel and connected with their heads and legs. They tucked in their tails and trotted off snarling. I'd gotten there just in the nick of time! The girl was bleeding from a few scratches, but otherwise she was all right. Her name was Lorin.

On the way back to the castle, she told me how her horse had sprained a leg on the way home from a visit to her aunt, and how on the difficult walk through the forest on foot she'd been set upon by the dogs. She'd really wanted to go falcon hunting that day, but her favorite falcon was off its feed, so instead she'd ridden to see her aunt, from whom she'd learned a new song. I told her that—even if I didn't look it—I was a squire, and that my Sir Frank was the bravest knight in the whole land. We chitchatted a little longer and parted when we came to the castle. Later I learned that Lorin was the duke's daughter! I could hardly believe it.

The tournament began.

The horses were led in. They were all decked out with coverings of costly stuffs. They danced nervously back and forth, so the grooms had trouble holding them. The knights, weighed down by their iron armor, had difficulty clambering up steps and ladders into their saddles.

The knights were dining in the large knights' hall. They sat at a long table at one end of the hall. Mountains of meat, bread, and pies were being brought in. The knights fell to with gusto. They drank beer and wine and were singing and laughing and bantering and squabbling. We squires might serve them, but only if we had fine, colorful clothes and shoes. Unfortunately I had neither fine clothes nor shoes, so I watched through the window.

In his mended clothes my Sir Frank looked very out of place in this company. His friends joked about it. Some big-mouthed knights who didn't know him poked fun at him with scornful or spiteful remarks. We didn't pay any attention; after the tournament, the laugh would be on them!

Finally the morning of the competition arrived. Huge platforms had been erected for the noblewomen of the duchy. In the center sat the duchess and the duke, ruler of all the land far and wide.

neighing, and the drumming of hundreds of hooves reverberated like a roll of thunder. Lances crashed against shields and helms. Some lances bent and split, riders tumbled from the saddle, wounded horses reared and threw their riders. The confusion was terrible. A thick cloud

Many a knight had fastened his lady's silken handkerchief to his helm or his arm for luck, a sign that he would fight to victory for the glory of his lady. Lances and shields shone with fresh paint. Horses pawed the ground impatiently. Never in my whole life had I seen anything so exciting!

The crowd of horsemen now divided into two groups, which positioned themselves opposite each other. Each rider was facing an opponent. At a sign from the duchess, accompanied by a trumpet flourish, the knights stormed at one another with lances in position. The horses were

of dust concealed much of the fighting from sight, but you could hear cries of pain and curses coming from it.

When the dust slowly settled, half the knights had been vanquished. For a moment I forgot my Sir Frank and the fighting, for I'd caught sight

This is our coat of arms

Some other coats of arms in the duchy

of Lorin! I saw her sitting on the platform, looking small and fragile. I waved wildly at her. She saw me and waved back, but in such a way that the stern ladies around her couldn't see her.

In the meantime the vanquished knights left the lists, some limping, others carried by their men. The victors got ready for the next contest. Again the trumpet sounded, again the earth shook under the hooves, and with each new round the number of fighters was decreased by half.

The guests of the duke and the duchess were placing bets on which knights would win. They didn't pay any attention to my Sir Frank. But he didn't care. He came through the first round brilliantly, easily removing his opponent from the saddle, for Tristrud was nimble and tough.

About noon the tourney was interrupted, and the duke invited everyone to a large midday meal. We squires also took our places at a long table and could eat as much as we wanted. It had been quite a time since I could do that! A loutish fellow named Rupp, red-haired and a squire like me, kept trying to take the best bits off my plate. I certainly was smaller, but therefore I was much faster. While he was snatching something from my plate, behind his back I quickly moved the food from his plate to mine. He tried to grab me, but I dodged out of his reach. The others were laughing, and they were on my side. After a time he gave up picking on me, but the look he threw me promised no good!

The tournament resumed after the noon meal. Now only twelve knights entered the lists. Such renowned knights as Max der Geier, Arno mit der eisernen Faust, Siegfried Rindsmaul, and even Beringer der Furchtbare had already been eliminated. Sir Frank von Fidelstein was not among the defeated.

The rules of the tournament were changed for the fight among the last six. Two knights at a time would now ride against each other, and not on the large field but right in front of the stands. A long timber barrier between the opponents would keep horses and riders from coming too close; only lances could cross the barrier. The first contest was won by Sir Löwenhaupt against Sir Gotthelf von Brausebach. In the next fight the knights clashed with such force that their lances bent and broke. Both knights were thrown from their horses. There was no victor. They

were carried from the field. In the third fight Sir Frank von Fidelstein connected so hard that the fierce Sir Tilsit sailed from his saddle. My heart was thumping like crazy!

Then the trumpets signaled the grand finale: Sir Löwenhaupt against Sir Frank von Fidelstein! There they came: the yellow knight on his strong, heavy horse and my Sir Frank von Fidelstein on our skinny Tristrud. My, he was strong! And as swift as a falcon!

In the breathless stillness the first clash sounded like a clap of thunder. With a skillful turn my Sir Frank lifted his opponent's lance from his arm. It flew through the air in a wide arc. But Sir Frank's own weapon was also broken at the same time. We squires brought new lances. The signal sounded, once again the two knights rushed at each other, and again my knight succeeded in parrying the terrible shock of the collision. Had this force hit him head on, he would have gone flying from the saddle!

The fifth pair of lances lay broken on the ground. New lances were brought, a new trumpet blast sounded. Both horses were exhausted. They could no longer be spurred to a full gallop. The clash of weapons was no longer so loud. Now the skill of my Sir Frank was proven, but so was the strength of Sir Löwenhaupt, whose nickname "the Invincible" was clearly deserved.

Both knights maintained their position, but the horses rose on their hind legs and threw the riders off. Bleeding and dirty, the two faced each

No one had believed that such a bony, thin frame possessed so much strength and skill. Astonishment was widespread. At the next passage of arms the famous, powerful knight Schwarz-zahn vom See was also vanquished—my Sir Frank flipped him out of his saddle. Schwarz-zahn is that loutish squire Rupp's knight. The knights who had so far survived the lists dipped their lances in front of the stand where the duke, the duchess, and the noble gentlemen and ladies, including Lorin, were sitting.

other. Applause broke out across the field. The knights had drawn their swords to finish the battle on foot. But then the duke rose and, accompanied by roars of joy from the crowd, awarded the victory to both. He didn't want to gamble with his good fortune in having two such magnificent fighters among his followers. The opponents embraced each other. They swore friendship, a friendship to endure from that day until death.

What happened next was sheer wild celebration. A banquet was prepared. Whole oxen, sheep, and pigs were roasted, kegs of beer and casks of wine were opened. The musicians tuned up, the jugglers juggled, and the dancers danced before the guests. We laughed and sang and ate and drank. This was a great day for me!

Through a window I could watch the awarding of prizes in the knights' hall. My knight got a shiny new helm and a second horse, whose name was Barbamusch. What made me happiest of all: My knight was given a stipend of two hundred silver marks a year. Now we wouldn't have to sleep outdoors anymore; every inn would be open to us. For however brave a knight may be, innkeepers still demand payment in advance. I turned a cartwheel for joy and was leaping around like a mountain goat.

It had gotten dark. Careless in my happiness, I jumped right out to the dark courtyard. All at once a great form came at me from the darkness; two paws that I knew only too well reached for me. I pulled back, but now many hands grabbed me and pulled me down. While fists hit me in the face and stomach like battering rams, I kept catching glimpses of Rupp's nasty grin. Colored stars and circles danced before my eyes, and then I must have passed out.

The first thing I saw after that was Lorin's worried face. She was wiping my face with a damp cloth. A maid had whispered to her what the uproar by the gate was about. She had sneaked away to come to me. After she'd splashed cold water in my face, I was fully awake again. My head ached terribly, but it hurt me even more to have been beaten up by that gang of lowdowns. We crept into a safe corner and began to plot revenge.

We considered how I could get at Rupp. He'd avoid me until he had his pals around him. And besides, at the moment I was much too feeble to fight him. What should I do? Should I arm myself? Then we heard Rupp and his gang bawling. They were celebrating their triumph over me with a lot of wine and braying. They were holed up in a room on the outer wall, which could only be reached by a bridge. The bridge had a slight slope to it. Lorin was laughing softly as she proposed a plan. "If we get some buckets of the slimy stink water from the back part of the moat where the kitchen garbage is thrown, and empty them over the bridge, anyone who comes out will slip and fall."

Lorin was simply fantastic! We got to work right away. It wasn't much fun to carry those disgusting pails, especially with my aching bones, but I wasn't doing it alone. We soon finished, and the entire bridge was slippery.

In a loud voice I began to jeer at Rupp. "Come out, if you dare, you red-haired slime of a waterbug. . . . You mouse behind . . . you quivering heap of fraud and dirty tricks, oh, you really stink of cowardice. Stink-Rupp, that's you! Stink-Rupp, who's scared out of his pants!"

That was too much for Squire Rupp. He charged out the door, crashed onto his back, and slid down the slanting bridge right at me.

I gathered all my strength and gave him a shove with my shoulder that threw him from the bridge. He landed some fifteen feet below on the uneven ground of the moat. Then the whole herd of brawlers poured out the door. They slipped, slid, and rolled toward us. We had our hands full sending them after Rupp, Lorin on the right side, I on the left. The first ones fell into the moat, the next ones on top of them. It was an enormous, gorgeous rout!

All at once we heard loud laughter from behind our backs. The knights and guests from the hall had been attracted by the noise and were enjoying our trick. We were hauled before the duke and duchess. They had a hard time hiding their smiles as they reproached their daughter for her combativeness. Of course Lorin was immediately led off to the ladies' apartments by the

stern aunts. But then her parents asked me for the story of the whole affair. As I stood before the duke, Sir Frank laid his hand protectingly on my shoulder. That he was standing up for me made me almost prouder than our victory in the tournament!

That night nothing could keep me awake, not any amount of noise or scratchy straw.

Sir Frank and I decided to stay at Castle Stolzenfels for a few days. We were famous people now—that is to say, of course Sir Frank was; you could more likely call me infamous. It's nice to be famous—as often as I came into the kitchen now, the nice fat cook would slip me a small or a large morsel of something delicious.

One morning I saw people running into the courtyard from every direction. A crowd gathered around a woman. She was hurt, and her clothes were in tatters. In the babble of voices I heard the words "attack" and "northern border."

The woman had been on the run from hordes of marauders for days and was begging for protection in the castle. The border patrol had brought her in.

Her news upset everyone. The quiet of the morning was gone, and now the place was buzzing like a nest of hornets. Mounted messengers were sent out to warn the villages, cloisters, and castles in the region. Sir Frank offered the duke our help, for our fortress lay so deep in the mountains that it was in no danger.

The duke took counsel with his knights in the great hall. Many people would be seeking asylum in the castle. New reports kept coming in from the spies and watches on the hills. Many, many miles away we could discern the path of the enemy by the fires and columns of smoke. All, even the knights, had to help make the castle ready. Above all the well had to be cleaned so that it would provide enough water for everyone to drink and for putting out fires.

The man-high battlements had to be repaired or renewed. They would protect the castle against the attackers' arrows and catapult missiles. A new defense gallery was built along the wall, from which we'd be better able to reach the attackers with hot pitch and with our weapons.

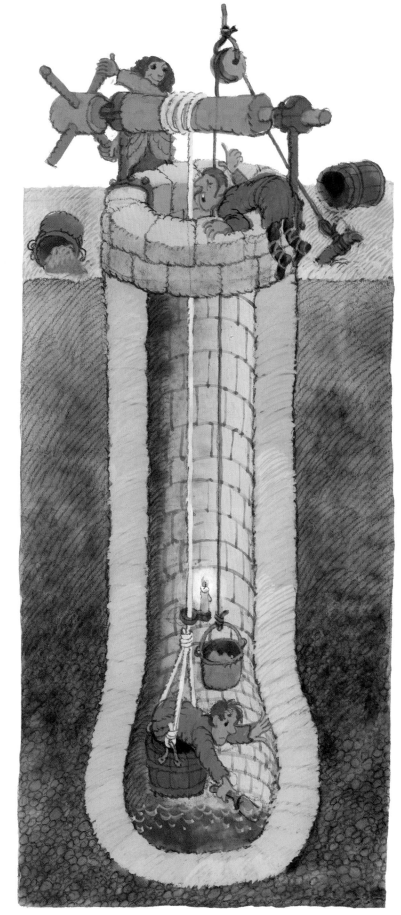

The wood of the drawbridge had rotted during the long period of peace and had to be replaced, because a raised drawbridge closes the entry to a castle and is the first line of defense against enemy arrows and battering rams. The points of the portcullis had to be sharpened.

The trophies of the hunt

Slain wild boar

Stag on a carrying pole

Pack of hounds —

Archery targets of straw

Dummy pheasant

Archery instructor

Lorin practicing —

Me

My first attempt

My Sir Frank had developed a new defense plan—stratagems and tricks to defend the castle against many attackers with only a few warriors. Thus we planned to fight with our wits and our strength, not with strength alone.

Tilting at a feisty dummy

—with a swinging punch

In peacetime the removable roofs protected the towers from the weather. Now we took them off. Since, like many who live in the mountains, I was not subject to dizziness, I clambered onto the roof like the duke's monkey to replace damaged roof tiles.

Weather protection

Whenever I had time, I practiced with weapons. I liked shooting with the bow and riding and fencing with the short sword best, especially because Lorin was often there doing it too. Her governesses didn't approve, but she knew the duke was secretly pleased, and that's why she was allowed to do it.

I also gathered wood for the watchfire, which burned all the time, and that took a lot of wood. We dragged pitch and oil up onto the ramparts until my shoulders and knees were numb.

The kettles for boiling pitch and oil were refurbished and some new ones made. We'd pour their boiling contents down on the attackers through the holes we call machicolations.

Lorin was getting better and better with weapons, so she wasn't easy to beat anymore. She was a very unusual girl! Whenever she could escape the governesses, we sat together and chatted. She told me of the life of the great castle. The family gathered before the fire in the evening. People sat on the colorful carpets from the Orient and, in the warm light of many candles, they listened to the stories and songs of the Minnesingers. Minnesingers are knights, but they conquer with poems, songs, and the lute as well as with weapons.

Lorin told me about the heralds, who can tell by the weapons whether a knight is qualified for tournament. She knew about secret herbs and medicines that can heal. She learned about that from her mother. She knew the news from foreign lands, and she knew poetry in a foreign language. When I marveled at how much she knew, she said, "While you men fight against our enemies, we women have time to beautify the castle and read and collect knowledge."

Then I told her about my parents' small estate and how I came to Sir Frank. I described the impoverished castle, where people didn't even know what a candle was. We only had pine torches, which smoked painfully and made our eyes tear.

Our rooms were gloomy all winter long, the walls gave off a coldness that no tapestry could block. But I also described to her our boundless joy when finally the spring comes and flowers cover the bare ground. In the warm light of the sun we would sing and dance and feel like kings.

I told Lorin that a chain mail hauberk for my knight cost his estate's entire income for almost two years, and she told me about an uncle who build a castle with an eighty-fathom-deep well that cost as much as the whole rest of the castle. It was wonderful to sit and talk with Lorin!

Handcart

Strong fellows

The women rule over kitchen and cellar

A cart full of stones for missiles

Drink is brought in

Meat is preserved by salting

Water reserves are tucked away in many places

Herds of animals are driven into the castle

Flour and grain

Pigs

Sheep

Sheep dog

Meat for smoking in the chimney

All the foodstuffs are assembled

Helper

Bellows

Spear shafts

The smith

Maces

"Holy-water sprinklers"

Charcoal

helms

Sword blades

More and more refugees came into the castle. Every day it became more crowded and noisy. Oxcarts full of wood and stones for throwing were continually creaking and groaning into the courtyard. Day and night the smiths were hammering fit to make your ears ring.

The neighing, squealing, mooing, and baaing of the herds that were being collected reached to the farthest corner of the castle. Even Lorin was saying she couldn't sleep because of the clatter of weapons, the crying of children, scolding of cooks, and curses of soldiers. There was a heavy smell of animals and people lying over everything.

Finally, at the special request of my weapons instructor and Sir Frank, I was inducted into the Duke's Guard. My first day of duty, they wakened me shortly before midnight. I was still half asleep as I reeled through the long, dark passageways of the castle. My guardsman's outfit included a pair of shoes. I'd no idea that shoes could pinch so!

I shall never forget that morning when, for the first time, I was at my post in the lookout of Castle Stolzenfels keeping watch over its many sleeping inhabitants, knowing that Lorin was among them.

Slowly the eastern sky took on color. It grew brighter and brighter, and then at one stroke the red-golden ball of the sun came over the horizon. The broad, hilly land of the duchy lay at my feet. It was a glorious sight, but a fearsome one too, for the fires of the marauders told that they were near. I stood watch and wondered what the day would bring.

You know the rest of the story. My Sir Frank went on to fame and glory, and I became a knight and won a few good fights too— you know, you've heard it all in the songs of the Minnesingers. Oh, I could tell you more, certainly, but now it's time for us to stop. I promised your grandmother I'd join her in the garden, and you know how Lady Lorin hates to be kept waiting!

The great sword for two hands

Two-handed swordsmen

Practice helm

Padded practice coat

Practice with the shield

Wooden sword

Used practice target

The correct angle for the spear

He got you!

A Note from the Translator

Many of the names Ali Mitgutsch has given his characters have a meaning in German. (Most of the names we use today, if we go back far enough, originally had a meaning, but that's a different story.) Although they don't always sound as "right" in English as they do in German, it's more fun if you know the joke. Sometimes the meaning isn't so important as the way the names sound. The spellings in parentheses show you how to pronounce them pretty much the way Germans do. And there are a couple of helpful rules you can remember for all the German words you ever meet: *ei* is always sounded like the letter *i*, and *ie* is always sounded like the letter *e*—in other words, look at the second letter of the pair and use that as a guide; the letter *z* always sounds like *tz*, *v* always sounds like *f*, *w* sounds like *v*, and *s* usually sounds like *z*.

Riding over bars Lorin

My first try at jumping a bar!

Bar

Practice with the "holy-water sprinkler"

Fencing with the pole-ax and lance

Leather padding

von Fidelstein (fohn FEE del styne): Merry Stone

Wolflieb (VOLLF leeb): He tells you what it means himself

Stolzenfels (STOLTZ en felz): Proud Rock

Rupp (ROOP): Rude

Max der Geier (MOCKS dehr GUY er): Max the Hawk

Arno mit der eisernen Faust (AR no mit dehr EYE zer nen FOWST): Arno with the Iron Fist

Tristan Schmettermann (TRISS tahn SHMET ter mahn): Tristan Man-Smasher

Alfons von Schneckenstein (AHL fonz fohn SHNEK ken styne): Alfons of Snail-Stone

Siegfried Rindsmaul (ZEEG freed RINNDZ mowl): Siegfried Ox-Mouth

Beringer der Furchtbare (BEHR ring er dehr FOORKT bah reh): Beringer the Terrible

Schwartzzahn vom See (SHVARTZ zahn fohm ZAY): Black Tooth of the Lake

Löwenhaupt (LE[R] ven howpt): Lion-Head

Gotthelf von Brausebach (GOT helf fohn BROWZ eh bock): God's-Help of Babbling Brook

Names that merely sound nice: **Tristrud** (TRISS trood), **Tilsit** (TIL zit), **Barbamusch** (BARB ba moosh)

with arrow cover

of thick leather

Assault cart

Stone missile

The pan

Trigger

Ballista

Burning brushwood

Jugs of burning oil or pitch

Catapult

Stone missiles

Shooting from cover

Poles for raising

Sturdy wheels

Siege tower On its side fo

Ram head of metal

Mantlet (portable arrow shield)